The sad song of the sea

A story writtin by Zawi El ouaamari

© Zawi El ouaamari

E-Mail: z_elouaamari@web.de

Printed and published by
BoD - Books on Demand, Norderstedt
ISBN 978-3-7460-4298-5

Foreword

Most people in the Third World and particularly in Africa are poor and feel unfairly treated by their governments. When they take to the streets to protest peacefully and publicly about their desperate situation, they are branded either as terrorists, or are stigmatized as anarchists.

As for example the demonstrations in Rif, a region in the north of Morocco: for more than a year **Nasser Zafzafi** and his friends have organized a civilized exemplary popular movement, the harak. They demonstrate quite peacefully for their fundamental rights and complain about the political and economic mismanagement, but they are labelled as separatists by the king and his government instead of fulfilling their legitimate requirements.

The corrupt tyrant has also ordered his brutal police forces to mercilessly beat down the peaceful demonstrators and carry out mass arrest. In addition, houses are being stormed and lawyers intimidated such as **Mr. El Bouchtaoui**, they only want to defend the innocent activists that are captured. Moreover, the Moroccan authorities are banning local and foreign journalists from reporting on this brutal and barbaric intervention by the police.

Consequently many of the people see only one way to escape from this miserable condition: to flee to Europe in order to have a better life there. They are willing to put out to sea, sometimes with a rubber dinghy, sometimes with a fishing boat. Their desperate attempt to come to Europe does not stop them from undertaking such a risky journey despite the danger of being drowned. Many people find death in the waves, only a few of them safely reach the European mainland.

The following story is about a young man from Husaima, a city in Rif, who came to Malaga as the only survivor, all the other twenty fleeing companions had drowned. They were all mutually helpful and nice to each other, not only during the period far out on sea, but also weeks earlier as they were waiting together for the people smuggler in a forest in the north of Morocco. But then the accident happened on the high seas, and everyone had to fight for their own survival …

Zafzafi

Thus spoke Zafzafi
Honour is a high quality
In the heart of the Rifi
Feels hotter than a glow

We want only justice
Are fully focus on it
That is all we require
It benefits you and us

Gold and silver are enough
So give us a part of them
Then you act sensibly
And we bury the hatchet

We are not separatists
Of that you accuse us
And we are tried of having
To justify ourselves constantly

Frankfurt on main, friday 22.02. 2018

Chapter 1, the tragedy on high seas

Ahmad was 16-year-old, he lived with his parents in **Husaima**. He was a slim young man but a slightly muscular, he had short black hair which lay in light frizzy waves, and brown eyes that revealed a smart and curious mind. Indeed Ahmad was a good student, but when his father fell seriously ill, he had to help his uncle in the parental grocery store. His previous good marks began to deteriorate, and he lost all pleasure in learning.

Hakim was an elder friend, he was now working as a human smuggler which displeased Ahmad, but he did not want to criticize his friend, especially as he did not see him for a long time.

Hakim often came to the store and tried to encourage his friend to run off to Europe. He deliberately visited Ahmad at the time when his uncle was not in the shop with the firm intention to tell him calmly about the beautiful and happy life in this continent. Initially he did not have any success to convince his friend with his sweet talk: on one hand the boy had no money, on the other hand he was too young to undertake such an adventure. Then the harak broke out in his city, since the day the boy increasingly felt the need to leave the corrupt country, and he started thinking about a marvellous life beyond the sea.

A small fishing boat, crowded with people, was hit hard by huge waves. It swung perilously back and forth for a while, until it was capsized by the next stronger wave, and broke into several parts. With the exception of Ahmad, all the others companions perished at sea. The young man swam to the nearest boards, with all the force he could muster in his body. He wanted to reach them before he got tired or they were driven off downstream with the strong current. He felt his death were close, and he seemed to clutch at straws.

Meanwhile the waves became weaker but still able to lift Ahmad upwards, when they rose, he saw the contours of a coast, and he tried with all his strength to swim to the shore. But when the waves moved downwards the boy feared to drown, before he could reach the cost, then he summoned up the courage and caught firmly the big and thick wooden board. Fortunately, the sea now became quiet. Ahmad slid over the board, laid down on his stomach, and began to row with hands and feet...

Chapter 2, the Schmitt´s

The Schmitt´s were a German married couple, who lived in Frankfurt. They had known each other since their childhood at school, where they used to sit together. The man was called Dieter, he was stocky and had slightly short grey hair, his light blue eyes gleamed behind thin glasses. He was not the stereotypical cool and reserved type, but more sympathetic and communicative guy. Dieter was an orientalist, he spoke standard Arabic and Spanish and had taught at the Goethe University.

His wife was called Andrea, she was an attractive, full-figured woman and had long light blond hair that fell to her shoulders. Her lovely green eyes and her charming face with speckled freckles had maintained her beautiful appearance despite her advanced age. Andrea was a doctor for general medicine and had a practise in her own house. She spoke French and Spanish. God had not given the both any children, they had tried to adopt a child three times, but their attempt failed every time due to strict German bureaucracy. As a result they were tired of the system, and they finally gave up this desire.

After the Schmitt´s had reached the retirement age, they sold their big and comfortable villa in Frankfurt and moved to Spain, where they bought a charming little house in a town near Malaga.

The house was situated secluded at the foot of a mountain behind a boulder that seemed like a natural wall. The view was idyllic: from the bathroom and the bedroom one saw the wonderful mountains and hills that were covered with a picturesque forest, and from the living room and bedroom the windows looked out onto the wide beautiful blue sea and a little port where many small ships and fishing boats ran in and out. Moreover, one could also see a winding country road. Further a military airfield was in the immediate surroundings where several times throughout the day helicopters started and landed.

Dieter was a poet and his wife a painter, when they were ready with their daily duties and important house activities, they lost themselves in their respective artistic inspirations: the man tried to capture the many experiences and impressions of life in words and the woman did that in paintings. The wide sea, the forest, the mountains, and all the beauty and charm of nature offered them plenty of creative inspirations, and so happy the Schmitt's spent their twilight years.

Chapter 3, Ahmad reached the coast

As soon as Ahmad had reached the cost, he ran to a rock. He set on warm sand, leaned against the rock, and breathed deeply in and out. He was very tired, but he could not sleep because dreadful thoughts now pursued him, it was barely tangible for him to be still alive.

His eyes wandered over the sea and then fixed on a spot where he thought he had escaped death.

About an hour later a military helicopter appeared in the blue sky, Ahmad was lost in these awful thoughts so that he did not notice the aircraft flying towards him, it was only his unbearable noise that interrupted his thoughts. The young man got a fright, he quickly got up, and he ran and hid behind the rock.

After the machine had flown away and disappeared in the distance, Ahmad climbed on top of the rock. He hoped to discover someone in the nearness who could give him water and some food.

Moreover, he hoped with his youthful naivety to find somebody offering him work and a home, but no one could be seen. Meanwhile the thirst became stronger and Ahmad definitely had to find water, he looked down in the valley then around him, there were mountains covered with a forest. After a few meters, the flat fine sandy beach turned into a gravelled surface similar to a wide rough carpet, and it gradually rose to a country road that appeared like a thick silver-grey snake.

The boy climbed down the rock, crossed the road, and disappeared into the forest. He was very lucky as he soon caught a sight of a stream in his immediate nearness and he ran there. The fresh water trickled down a boulder and flowed into a small pond, Ahmad stretched his hands, took out some scoops of water and he drank with great gulps until he quenched his burning thirst.

The youngster went in search of a safe place where he could calmly dry his clothes. He had walked about a quarter of an hour when he came into a clearing bordered to the edge of the mountain where a thick tree stood majestically apart. Ahmad took off his trousers and shirt, laid them on the grass in the sun, and sat down in shadow under the tree. He removed the plastic bag from his chest, took out the bank notes, and began to wag them in order to generate a little coolness.

After his clothes became dry, he put them on and set out. The boy walked for a while, and suddenly he heard an incomprehensible voice, he stopped walking, then he went ducking down out of sight, hidden behind a vertical rock that seemed like a natural wall. Ahmad took a deep breath and then stretched his head trying to see who was behind the boulder. He clearly saw a man and a woman in front of a secluded house. It was the Schmitt´s: Dieter was standing and rotating a barbecue, and Andrea was sitting and cutting bread.

The smell of the crispy meat on a spear over the low flames wafted towards the boy in the gentle breeze making him more hungry, and his stomach began to rumble. He had not eaten for two days, the last meal he took was a piece of bread and some dates when he was on the boat. However, he did not want to go to this people and ask them for some food for fear they might deliver him to the police.

He went ducking further and he soon saw that the path bent and ended at the house, in that moment he did not watch out for a steep slope so he slipped, lost his balance, and fell to the side. His left foot was twisted and he involuntary let out a loud scream then he clenched the teeth and tried to suppress the pain, however, the foot hurt in such a way that he began to shout for help. Ahmad now sat at a dangerous, steep place where a slight movement sufficed to plunge into the depths.

Dieter and Andrea saw the boy, they clearly heard his cries for help and they hurried towards him. With great effort they carefully pulled him up and brought him into the guest room, Dieter helped him to lay on the bed. Andrea put on a pair of protective gloves and took off his plastic sandals, and after making sure that he had any fractures on his legs and his feet, she disinfected the scratches and washed the bloodstains with a special liquid, sprayed a painkiller and dressed the wound.

Despite the great pain Ahmad could not turn his eyes away from the crispy and succulent meat that lay in slices in a large plate and seemed to smile at him. Andrea gave him a plate with some meat and bread and a glass of juice. Ahmad thanked her and then he began to eat, he chewed mechanically rather than consciously. Before he could even finish eating he fell into a deep sleep, the woman covered him with a thin blanket. Then she switched off the light, went out of the room, and shut the door.

Chapter 4, the change of mind

Already on the next day, Dieter drove to Malaga and sent a message in French to the parents of Ahmad that their son had safely reached Spain and they should not worry because he was in good hands with them. He also bought for the boy some summer clothes, and personal care products, and a pair of sandals.

Two weeks had passed and Ahmad's foot was now fully recovered and he felt much better and could walk painlessly. However, for his own safety he was only allowed to walk around the house and in the garden, he went only in the afternoon to the beach to have some change, the Schmitt´s knew at that time of day military helicopters did not fly around and there was no patrols.

One evening there was a storm, it was thundering and lightning, and the rain incessantly knocked at the shutters. After the Schmitt´s and Ahmed had finished dinner, they comfortably sit in the living room and watched TV. "Ahmad, imagine you have a million Euro, what will you do with it?", asked Dieter the young man abruptly. The boy was surprised, he looked at Andrea as if he asked her to answer for him.

"You said your father is very ill and he needs a lot of money for the medical treatment", replied the nice woman encouraging him, "So you could give him a part of a million for this."

"O yes, and I also give him some money to hire a worker for a few years so that I can go back to the school without any trouble", said Ahmad with relief.

"I remember a good advice of my uncle, he often told me if one day I became rich I should buy a large arable area of land for growing different types of edible plants and keeping livestock. He gave reasons for his words that in this way one always has something to eat when a crisis breaks out."

"Of course, a farm is a good option, but why don't you invest in gold and silver too?", asked Dieter with more likely a pedandic impression looking at the young man over the glasses. "Why should I do that?", replied he. "That's because the both precious metals together with property outlast every financial and economic crisis."

This short conversation was followed by a long silence, the thunderstorm had stopped, only small raindrops were rhythmic hitting against the shutters. At this moment Andrea wished the time might turn back to the years as she was a young woman and Ahmad still a child so that she could adopt him. The old desire flamed up and her beautiful eyes filled with tears, Dieter was conscious of the heartbreaking emotions through which his wife now went, he knew them very well: whenever children came close to her for a long time she was overwhelmed by the old feeling that she could not get children. And as soon as she was alone, Andrea could not control her feelings any more, she began to sob and then she burst into tears. Her husband tried to comfort her, but it took a while before she calmed down.

Ahmad got up earlier than usual and went to the beach, he searched for a safety place where he could not discovered by the gendarmerie, and he soon found such one. He set on a rock and looked out down to the wide sea, it was quite and seemed like a blue carpet that extended to the horizon. He gazed into the distance, of course he could not see beyond the horizon but he knew what was there: his parents, his brothers and sisters, his uncle, his relatives, his friends, he nearly would have drowned before he could have seen them again, only now was he aware of the extent of the disaster. He saw how his boat companions were torn by high waves, they were on brink of drowning, he heard them crying for help as if it now happened.

"Why this damn business!?", shouted the boy suddenly and ran away, it was very sad to see him in such a helpless situation.

After a long discussion, the Schmitt´s decided to support Ahmad financially. But this help was on one condition: with the money that the both would send every month, Ahmad's father should have to hire a worker in the shop so that his son could return to school, moreover, Dieter and Andrea would regularly visit Morocco in order to control locally the development of their support. Ahmad cordially thanked this nice people, he was overjoyed with this news and it gave him great happiness.

The Schmitt's made a decision to initiate this arrangement as soon as possible. Indeed, they took with Ahmad a few days later the ferry to Morocco. It was a late summer day, the weather was beautiful with the picturesque scenery around, the laughing sun and the blue sky.

After the travellers had gone on board, the ship ran out, and his prow began to divide the waves, it seemed as if a plough were digging furrows into the ground and clods fell apart.
Andrea, Dieter and Ahmad were leaning against the railing and gazing into the distance, the coast was now out of sight and there was nothing to be seen except the majestic blue sky which arched over the quiet nevertheless awe-inspiring water mass. Suddenly Dieter took a piece of paper out of his pocket and began to read his new poem which he had written to the occasion of the Ahmad's sad experience and generally about the danger on open sea.

The sad song of the sea

O describe me the wide sea
The victory over every army!

The waves spit white foam
They lick smoothly the rock
Silvery shining in sunlight
This is a beautiful view!

O describe me the wide sea
The victory over every army!

Nothing to see under the sky
No grass, no mountain, no tree
But a wavy field of water
Running up to the horizon

O describe me the wide sea
The victory over every army!

Thoughts ride on the waves
Eager with unseen ladles
to get secrets from the depth
Which so long sleep in it

O describe me the wide sea
The victory over every army!

Of haughty people they perished
They believed to be powerful
So they tried to outwit the sea
But they tumble down and drowned

O describe me the wide sea
The victory over every army!

And secrets of sad people
They wanted to be happy
Beyond all kinds of misery
However they paid with life

O describe me the wide sea
The victory over every army!

When the waves begin to rage
And there is around no escape
One is worrying about his life
And is ready to give all for it

O describe me the wide sea
The victory over every army!

And when they calm down
And though one comes ashore
Nevertheless he crouches startled
As if he were still in their clutches

O describe me the wide sea
The victory over every army!

Say you horrible water grave
How many have you swallowed?
And how many are still riding
Them you have lured with wealth?

Chapter 5, Ahmed in the classroom

All thanks were due to the nice German couple, they had solved the financial problem of the family of Ahmed, and now the obstacles that prevented the boy from continuing the school were cleared away.

One morning the Arabic teacher wrote a historical sentence from Tariq´s famous speech[1] on the blackboard: "The sea is behind you and the enemy in front of you", and underlined it. He looked at the students for a while, then he asked Ahmad to analyse grammatically this group of words.

"Teacher, the meaning of the sentence doesn't make any sense and it must be corrected."

"Hmm, tell me what's wrong with it then", requested the teacher smiling.

---

[1] Tariq ibn Ziyad was the Moroccan commander who conquered Spain in 711 AD.

"Things have changed, teacher, so that a former foe has become a friend and a friend an enemy, thus the pain and torture are now behind us and the grace and human dignity in front of us. It is our own people who are harassing us and taking away every means of existence so that we are forced to leave our homeland. May I continue talking, teacher?"

"Of course Ahmad, please go ahead."

"What reasonable person voluntarily leaves his country and his family if he has a little of human dignity and the possibility to lead a happy life? We hear every day of the pitiful people who risk their lives riding on the waves, and many of them finaly drown. Why do the scholars preach that the oppressed people should not protest against the unjust governments as long as they say their prayers? But it doesn't make any sense if the prayer doesn't restrain from doing turpitude? And is there any greater turpitude than injustice not only towards the Muslims, but towards all human beings? Have The scholars forgotten that the heavens and the earth were only built in truth and justice, why don't they admonish their governments to protect the rights of the citizens? You asked me, teacher, to express how are the words in the sentence grammatically arranged, but I tell you what I have in mind and what it stirs my emotions. Glory be to Allah who has given to the human beings the ability to combine grammatically words forming a sentence, to explain the connection between each other and to express all that we feel and think about!"

Annex

Here is the meaning of some words mentioned in the story:

admonish to gently tell someone that they have done something wrong

adopt to legally become the parents of someone else's child

adventure an exciting and sometimes dangerous experience

advice suggestions about what you think someone should do or how they should do something

aircraft a vehicle that can fly

airfield a place where small or military aircraft can take off and land

analyse to examine the details of something carefully, in order to understand or explain it

anarchist someone who thinks that society should not be controlled by a government and laws

appearance the way a person or thing looks

arrangement an agreement between two people or groups

ashore onto land from the sea, a river, a lake, etc

arrest if the police arrest someone, they take them away to ask them about a crime which they might have committed

attempt when you try to do something

authority the official power to make decisions or to control other people

aware be aware of/that to know about something

awe-inspiring causing people to feel great respect or admiration

to be banning is the gerund of to ban meaning to officially say that someone must not do something

barbaric violent and cruel

barbecue a party at which you cook food over a fire outdoors or a metal frame for cooking food over a fire outdoors

barely only just possible

beyond on the other side of something

blackboard a large board with a dark surface that teachers write on with chalk

blanket a thick, warm cover that you sleep under

bloodstain a mark or spot of blood

boulder a very large rock

brand to describe someone or something in a way that makes them seem bad

breeze a gentle wind

brink to be on the brink of sth to be in a situation where something bad is going to happen very soon

bureaucracy complicated rules and processes used by an organization, especially when they do not seem necessary

capsize If a boat capsizes, or if it is capsized, it turns over in the water

carpet thick material for covering floors, often made of wool

charming pleasant or attractive

clearing a small area in the middle of a forest, where there are no trees

clench to close your hands or teeth very tightly, or to hold something tightly

climb to go up something, or onto the top of something

clod a piece of soil or clay

clutch to hold something tightly

complain to say that something is wrong or that you are annoyed about something

be conscious of/that to know that something is present or that something is happening

consequently as a result

contour the shape of the outer edge of something

convince to make someone believe that something is true

cordially adverb relating to the adjective polite and friendly

crispy food is pleasantly hard and easy to bite through

crouch to move your body close to the ground by bending your knees

crowded very full of people

curious wanting to know or learn about something

current happening or existing now

damn used to express anger

deliberately intentionally, having planned to do something

deliver to take things such as letters, parcels, or goods to a person or place

despite used to say that something happened or is true, although something else makes this seem not probable

deteriorate to become worse

digging/ dig to break or move the ground with a tool, machine, etc

dignity calm and serious behaviour that makes people respect you

dinghy a small boat

disaster something that causes a lot of harm or damage

discover to find something

downstream in the direction that the water in a river is moving in

drown to die because you are under water and cannot breathe, or to kill someone in this way

eager wanting to do or have something very much

estate a large area of land in the countryside that is owned by one person

fear a strong, unpleasant feeling that you get when you think that something bad, dangerous, or frightening might happen

ferry a boat that regularly carries passengers and vehicles across an area of water

field an area of land used for growing crops or keeping animals

firm certain or fixed and not likely to change

flame hot, bright, burning gas produced by something on fire

flee to leave a place quickly because you are in danger or are afraid

flow if something such as a liquid flows, it moves somewhere in a smooth, continuous way

floam a mass of small, white bubbles on the surface of a liquid

foe an enemy

foreign belonging to or coming from another country, not your own

forest a large area of trees growing closely together

foreword a short piece of writing at the front of a book that introduces the book or its writer

fracture to break something hard such as a bone, or a piece of rock

freckled covered with very small, brown spot on your skin from the sun

fright a sudden feeling of shock and fear

frizzy small tight stiff curls

front close to the front part of something

fulfilling/ fulfil to do something that you have promised to do or that you are expected to do

furrow a deep line cut into a field that seeds are planted in

gaze at/into to look for a long time at someone or something or in a particular direction

generating / generate to cause something to exist

gentle not strong or severe

gleam to shine in a pleasant, soft way

glory when people praise and respect you for achieving something important

glove a piece of clothing which covers your fingers and hand

government the group of people who officially control a country

grace the quality of being pleasantly polite

gradually slowly over a period of time

grammatically adverb relating to the adjective grammatical that means obeying the rules of grammar

grave a place in the ground where a dead body is buried

gravelled participle from small pieces of stone used to make paths and road surfaces

grocery a shop that sells food and products used in the home

gulp a noun relating to drink or eat something quickly, also gulp down

guy a man

harass to continue to annoy or upset someone over a period of time

haughty showing that you think you are much better or more important than other people

hid to put something in a place where it cannot be seen or found

hill a raised area of land, smaller than a mountain

hire to begin to employ someone

hit to touch something quickly and with force using your hand or an object in your hand

homeland the country where you were born

horizon the line in the distance where the sky seems to touch the land or sea

horrible very unpleasant or bad

however used to say that it does not make any difference

huge extremely large
a huge house

hurried / hurry to move or do things more quickly than normal or to make someone do this

hurt to cause someone pain or to injure them

idyllic an idyllic place or experience is extremely pleasant, beautiful, or peaceful

immediate happening or done without waiting or very soon after something else

impression an idea, feeling, or opinion about something or someone

incessantly adverb relating to the adjective incessant that means continuous, especially in a way that is annoying or unpleasant

incomprehensible impossible to understand

increasingly more and more

indeed used to add emphasis after very followed by an adjective or adverb

initially at the beginning

initiate to make something begin

injustice a situation or action in which people are treated unfairly

inspiration a (sudden) good idea about what you should do

instead adverb in the place of someone or something else

intention something that you want and plan to do

intervention when someone intervenes, especially to prevent something from happening

intimidate to intentionally frighten someone, especially so that they will do what you want

invest to give money to a bank, business, etc, or buy something, because you hope to get a profit

involuntary an involuntary movement or action is something you do but cannot control

knock to make a noise by hitting something, especially a door

label to describe the qualities of someone or something using a word or phrase, usually in a way that is not fair

ladle a large, deep spoon, used to serve soup

lawyer someone whose job is to understand the law and deal with legal situations

legitimate allowed by law

lick to move your tongue across the surface of something

lift to put something or someone in a higher position

loud making a lot of noise

lure to persuade someone to go somewhere or do something by offering them something exciting

maintain to make a situation or activity continue in the same way

majestic very beautiful or powerful in a way that people admire

marvellous extremely good

meanwhile in the time between two things happening, or while something else is happening

mechanically if you do something mechanically or in a mechanical way, you do it without emotion or without thinking about it

misery great suffering or unhappiness

mismanagement when something is badly organized or controlled

moreover also

muscular having firm, strong muscles
muscular legs/arms

muster to get enough support, bravery, or energy to do something difficult

mutually you use mutually before an adjective when the adjective describes all sides of a situation

naivety he quality of being naive

nevertheless adverb despite that

nodded past tense of to nod which means to move your head up and down as a way of agreeing, to give someone a sign, or to point to something

obstacle something that makes it difficult for you to go somewhere or to succeed at something

occasion a time when something happens

oppressed past tense of to oppress which means to treat a group of people in an unfair way, often by limiting their freedom

orientalist a European expert in eastern languages and cultures

outlast to continue for longer than someone or something else

outwit to get an advantage over someone by doing something clever and deceiving them

overjoyed very happy

parental involving or provided by parents

patrol a group of soldiers or vehicles that patrol an area or building

pedandic thinking too much about details and rules

perilously adverb relating to the adjective very dangerous

perished (literary) died

picturesque a picturesque place is attractive to look at.

piteously adverb relating to pity

pitiful adjective relating to pity

plough UK (US **plow**) a large tool used by farmers to turn over the soil before planting crops, or to turn over soil with a plough

pond a small area of water

port a town or an area of a town next to water where ships arrive and leave from

prayer the words you say to God

preach to talk to a group of people about a religious subject, usually as a priest in a church

precious very important to you

prevent to stop something happening or to stop someone doing something to prevent accidents/crime

prow when you are good at doing something

pursue to follow someone or something, usually to try to catch them

quenched to drink liquid so that you stop being thirsty

quiet without much noise or activity

quite a little or a lot but not completely

rage strong anger that you cannot control

railing a fence made from posts and bars

reasonable fair and showing good judgment

recover to become healthy or happy again after an illness, injury, or period of sadness

relative a member of your family

relief the good feeling that you have when something unpleasant stops or does not happen

replied past tense of to reply which means to answer

requested past tense of to request which means to ask politely or officially for something

requirement something that is needed or demanded

respective relating to each of the people or things that you have just talked about

restrain to stop someone doing something, sometimes by using force

retirement when you leave your job and stop working, usually because you are old

revealed past tense of to reveal which means to give someone a piece of information that is surprising or that was previously secret

rhythmic adjective relating to rhythm which means a regular, repeating pattern of sound

rotating turning in a circular direction

rough a rough surface is not smooth

row to move a boat or move someone in a boat through the water

rumble to make a deep, long sound

scenery the attractive, natural things that you see in the countryside

scholar someone who has studied a subject and knows a lot about it

scoop to remove something from a container using a spoon, your curved hands, etc

scratch a slight cut or a long, thin mark made with a sharp object

scream o make a loud, high noise with your voice, or to shout something in a loud, high voice because you are afraid, hurt, or angry

secluded if a place is secluded, it is quiet and not near people

sense a meaning or reason that you can understand

sentence a group of words, usually containing a verb, that expresses a complete idea

shadow a dark area made by something that is stopping the light

shore the area of land along the edge of the sea or a lake

shout to say something very loudly

shutter a wooden or metal cover on the outside of a window

slice a flat piece of food that has been cut from a larger piece

slid past tense of to silde which means to move smoothly over a surface, or to make something move smoothly over a surface

slight small and not important

slightly a little

slipped past tense of to slip which means o slide by accident and fall or almost fall

slope a surface or piece of land that is high at one end and low at the other

smart intelligent

smell to have a particular quality that people notice by using their nose

smoothly adverb from adjective smooth which means having a regular surface that has no holes or lumps in it

smouldering o have a strong feeling, especially anger, but not express it

smuggler someone who takes things
into or out of a place in an illegal or secret way

snake a long, thin creature with no legs that slides along the ground

sob to cry in a noisy way

solved past tense of to solve which means to find the answer to something

spear a long weapon with a sharp point at one end used for hunting

speckled covered in a pattern of very small spots

spit to force out the liquid in your mouth

spot a small, round mark which is a different colour to the surface it is on

spray liquid in a container which forces it out in small drops

startle to suddenly surprise or frighten someone

steep a steep slope, hill, etc goes up or down very quickly

stereotypical having the qualities that you expect a particular type of person to have

stigmatized to treat someone or something unfairly by disapproving of them

stir to make someone feel a strong emotion

stocky having a wide, strong, body

stomach the organ inside your body where food is digested

storm very bad weather with a lot of rain, snow, wind, etc

straw the long, dried stems of plants such as wheat

stream a small river

strength when someone or something is strong

stretch to make your body or part of your body straighter and longer

strong person or animal is physically powerful

succulent food that is good to eat because it has a lot of juice

summon to make a great effort to do something

suppress to control feelings so that they do not show

surroundings he place where someone or something is and the things that are in it

swallow to move your throat in order to make food or drink go down

tangible something which is tangible is real and can be seen, touched, or measured

torture severe pain caused to someone often in order to make him tell something

trickled if liquid trickles somewhere, it flows slowly and in a thin line

tumble to suddenly fall

turpitude behaviour that is dishonest or immoral

twilight the time just before it becomes completely dark in the evening, but the twilight years means the rest of live

tyrant someone who has total power and uses it in a cruel and unfair way

unbearable too painful or unpleasant for you to continue to experience

undertake to start work on something that will take a long time or be difficult

vertical pointing straight up from a surface

voluntarily adverb relating to the adjective voluntary which means done or given because you want to and not because you have been foreced to

wafted when a smell gradually moves through the air

wag to move something from side to side

youngster a young person, especially an older child

The following list contains all words in the story - without repetition - arranged in alphabetical order:

able about accident activists activities addition admonish adopt advanced adventure advice Africa after afternoon again against age aircraft airfield alive all allowed alone already also an analyse anarchists and answer any apart appearance appeared Arabic arched are army around arrangement arrest artistic as ashore ask asked at attempt attractive authorities aware away awe-inspiring awful back bag balance bank banning barbaric barbecue barely bathroom be beach beat beautiful beauty became because become bed bedroom before began begin behind being beings believed below beneath bent better beyond big black blackboard blanket, blond bloodstains blue board boards, boat boats body bordered both bought boulder boy branded bread breaking breath breathed breeze brink broke brothers brought brown brutal build built bureaucracy burning business but buy by called calm calmed calmly came can capsized captured care carefully carpet carry caught change changed chapter charm charming chest, chewed child childhood children citizens city civilized classroom cleared clearing clearly clenched climbed clods close closely clothes clutch clutches coast come comes comfort comfortable comfortably communicative companions complain condition conscious consciously Consequently content continent continue continuing contours control conversation convince cool coolness cordially corrected corrupt cost, could country couple, courage course covered creative cries crisis crispy criticize crossed crouches crowded cry, crying curious current cutting daily damn danger dangerous dates day days, dear death decided deep deeply defend definitely deliberately deliver demonstrate demonstrations demonstrators depth depths describe desire desperate despite deteriorate, development did digging dignity dinghy, dinner, disappeared disaster discover discovered discussion, disinfected displeased distance, divide do doctor does doesn't don't door down downstream downwards drank dreadful dressed drew driven drove drown drowned drowning, dry ducking due during duties each eager earlier earth eat, eaten eating economic edge effort either elder emotions encourage encouraging ended enemy escape especially estate Euro, Europe European even evening every everyone example except exception exemplary existence experience experiences express expressed expression extended extent eyes face failed family famous far farm father fear feared feel feelings feet, feet... fell felt ferry few field fight filled finally financial financially find fine finish finished firm first fishing fixed flamed flames flat flee fleeing

flowed flown fly flying foam foe
followed following food foot for force
forced forces foreign forest foreword
forgotten form former forth Fortunately,
found fractions Frankfurt freckles
French fresh friend friends fright, frizzy
from front fulfilling fully function
fundamental furrows further garden,
gave gaze gendarmerie, general
generally generating gentle German get
give given glass glasses gleamed Glory
gloves go God gold gone good got
government governments grace
gradually grammatically grass grave
gravelled great greater green grey grip
grocery ground guest gulps guy had hair
hand hands, happened happiness happy
harassing hard has haughty have he
head hear heard heart heavens
helicopter helicopters help helped
helpful helpless her hid hidden high
hills him hire his hit hitting Hmm, home,
homeland hoped horizon horrible hour
house how however huge human
hungry hurl hurried hurt husband idyllic
if ill imagine, immediate important

impression impressions in incessantly incomprehensible increasingly indeed initially initiate injustice inspirations instead intention interpretation interrupted intervention intimidated into invest involuntary journalists journey juice justice king knew knocked known labelled laid landed large last late laughing lawyers lay lead leaned learning leave left legitimate legs let lick life lift light like line liquid little lived lives living local locally long looked looking lost lot loud lovely low lucky lured machine mainland maintained majestic majestically make makes making Malaga man many marks married marvellous mass may me, meal meaning meanings means meanwhile meat mechanically medical medicine mercilessly message metals meters might military million mind miserable misery mismanagement moment money month, more moreover morning Moroccan Morocco most mountain moved movement much muscular Muslims, must muster mutually my naivety Nasser natural nature near nearest nearly nearness need needs nevertheless new news next nice nodded noise north not notes nothing notice now obstacles occasion of off offered offering often old on once one only onto open oppressed or order ordered organized orientalist other our out outlast outwit over overjoyed own paid pain painkiller painlessly painter, paintings pair paper parents part particularly parts passed paternal path patrols peaceful peacefully pedandic people perilously period perished person personal picturesque piece piteously pitiful place plastic plate please pleasure plenty plough plump pocket poem poet police political pond poor popular port possibility possible powerful practise prayer prayers preach precious prevented problem products, protect protective protest prow publicly pulled pursued put quarter quenched quickly quiet quite rage railing rain raindrops ran rather reach reached read ready real reasonable recovered regard region regularly related, relatives, relief remember removed replied reporting requested requirements reserved respective restrain result retirement return revealed rhythmic rich ride riding rights risk risky road rock room rose rotating rough row rubber rumble, run sad sadness safe safely safety said sand, sandals sandy sat saw say scenery scholars school scoops scratches scream sea search searched secluded second secrets see seemed seen seized send sense senses sent sentence sentences separatists seriously set several shadow she shining ship ships shirt, shop shore short should shoulders shout shouted show shows shut shutters side sight silence, silver silver-grey silvery similar since sisters, sit sitting situated situation sky, sleep slender slices slid slight slightly slipped, slope small smart smell smile smiling smoothly smouldering smuggler snake So so so-called sob sold solved some somebody someone sometimes son song soon Spain Spanish spear special speckled speech spent spit spoke spot sprayed standard standing stared started startled steep stereotypical stigmatized still stirs stocky stomach stood stop stopped store stormed story straws stream streets strength stretched strict strong stronger strongly student, success succulent such suddenly summer summoned sun sunlight support suppress sure surface surprised surroundings survival survivor, swallowed swam sweet swim switched swung sympathetic syntactic system, taking talk talking tangible taught teacher, tears, teeth tell terrorists, than thanked thanks that the their them themselves then there these they thick thin thing thinking third thirst this though thought thoughts three through throughout thundered thunderstorm thus time tired to together told too took top torn torture towards town tragedy travellers treated treatment tree trickled tried trouble trousers trowels truth try tumble turn turned turpitude twenty twilight twisted two type tyrant unbearable uncle under undertake undertaking unfairly university unjust unseen until up uphill upwards, us used usual valley value vertical very vessel, victory view villa visit visited voice, voluntarily wafted wag waiting walk walked walking, wall wander wandered want wanted warm was washed watch water wave wavy way weaker wealth weather weeks well went were what when whenever where which while white who why wide wife willing winding windows wished with without woman wonderful wooden words work worker working world worried worry would wound written wrong wrote year years yes you young youngster your youthful